THE WELL OF THE SAINTS

By the Same Writer

THE ARAN ISLANDS
Illustrated by
Jack B. Yeats

THE PLAYBOY OF THE WESTERN WORLD

IN THE SHADOW OF THE GLEN

RIDERS TO THE SEA

THE TINKER'S WEDDING

DEIRDRE OF THE SORROWS

KERRY AND WICKLOW

POEMS AND TRANSLATIONS

THE WELL OF THE SAINTS

A Comedy in Three Acts

By J. M. SYNGE

JOHN W. LUCE & COMPANY
BOSTON : : : : : : : : : : : : 1911

THE WELL OF THE SAINTS

SCENE

Some lonely mountainous district in the east of Ireland one or more centuries ago.

PERSONS IN THE PLAY

MARTIN DOUL, *weather-beaten, blind beggar*

MARY DOUL, *his Wife, weather-beaten, ugly woman, blind also, nearly fifty*

TIMMY, *a middle-aged, almost elderly, but vigorous smith*

MOLLY BYRNE, *fine-looking girl with fair hair*

BRIDE, *another handsome girl*

MAT SIMON

THE SAINT, *a wandering Friar*

OTHER GIRLS AND MEN

THE WELL OF THE SAINTS

ACT I

Roadside with big stones, etc., on the right; low loose wall at back with gap near centre; at left, ruined doorway of church with bushes beside it. Martin Doul and Mary Doul grope in on left and pass over to stones on right, where they sit.

MARY DOUL. What place are we now, Martin Doul?

MARTIN DOUL. Passing the gap.

MARY DOUL — *raising her head.*— The length of that! Well, the sun's getting warm this day if it's late autumn itself.

MARTIN DOUL — *putting out his hands in sun.*— What way wouldn't it be warm and it getting high up in the south? You were that length plaiting your yellow hair you have the morning lost on us, and the people are after passing to the fair of Clash.

MARY DOUL. It isn't going to the fair, the time they do be driving their cattle and they with a litter of pigs maybe squealing in their carts, they'd give us a thing at all. (*She sits down.*) It's well you know that, but you must be talking.

MARTIN DOUL — *sitting down beside her and beginning to shred rushes she gives him.*— If I didn't talk I'd be destroyed in a short while listening to the clack you do be making, for you've a queer cracked voice, the Lord have mercy on you, if it's fine to look on you are itself.

MARY DOUL. Who wouldn't have a cracked voice sitting out all the year in the rain falling? It's a bad life for the voice, Martin Doul, though I've heard tell there isn't anything like the wet south wind does be blowing upon us for keeping a white beautiful skin — the like of my skin — on your neck and on your brows, and there isn't anything at all like a fine skin for putting splendour on a woman.

MARTIN DOUL — *teasingly, but with good humour.*— I do be thinking odd times we don't know rightly what way you have your splendour, or asking myself, maybe, if you have it at all, for the time I was a young lad, and had fine sight, it was the ones with sweet voices were the best in face.

MARY DOUL. Let you not be making the like of that talk when you've heard

Timmy the smith, and Mat Simon, and Patch Ruadh, and a power besides saying fine things of my face, and you know rightly it was "the beautiful dark woman" they did call me in Ballinatone.

MARTIN DOUL — *as before.*— If it was itself I heard Molly Byrne saying at the fall of night it was little more than a fright you were.

MARY DOUL — *sharply.*— She was jealous, God forgive her, because Timmy the smith was after praising my hair ——

MARTIN DOUL — *with mock irony.*— Jealous!

MARY DOUL. Ay, jealous, Martin Doul; and if she wasn't itself, the young and silly do be always making game of them that's dark, and they'd think it a fine thing if they had us deceived, the way we wouldn't know we were so fine-looking at all.

[*She puts her hand to her face with a complacent gesture.*

MARTIN DOUL — *a little plaintively.*— I do be thinking in the long nights it'd be a grand thing if we could see ourselves for one hour, or a minute itself, the way we'd know surely we were the finest man and the finest woman of the seven counties of the east —

(*bitterly*) and then the seeing rabble below might be destroying their souls telling bad lies, and we'd never heed a thing they'd say.

MARY DOUL. If you weren't a big fool you wouldn't heed them this hour, Martin Doul, for they're a bad lot those that have their sight, and they do have great joy, the time they do be seeing a grand thing, to let on they don't see it at all, and to be telling fool's lies, the like of what Molly Byrne was telling to yourself.

MARTIN DOUL. If it's lies she does be telling she's a sweet, beautiful voice you'd never tire to be hearing, if it was only the pig she'd be calling, or crying out in the long grass, maybe, after her hens. (*Speaking pensively.*) Itshould be a fine, soft, rounded woman, I'm thinking, would have a voice the like of that.

MARY DOUL — *sharply again, scandalized.*— Let you not be minding if it's flat or rounded she is; for she's a flighty, foolish woman, you'll hear when you're off a long way, and she making a great noise and laughing at the well.

MARTIN DOUL. Isn't laughing a nice thing the time a woman's young?

MARY DOUL — *bitterly.*— A nice thing

is it? A nice thing to hear a woman making a loud braying laugh the like of that? Ah, she's a great one for drawing the men, and you'll hear Timmy himself, the time he does be sitting in his forge, getting mighty fussy if she'll come walking from Grianan, the way you'll hear his breath going, and he wringing his hands.

MARTIN DOUL — *slightly piqued.*— I've heard him say a power of times it's nothing at all she is when you see her at the side of you, and yet I never heard any man's breath getting uneasy the time he'd be looking on yourself.

MARY DOUL. I'm not the like of the girls do be running round on the roads, swinging their legs, and they with their necks out looking on the men. . . . Ah, there's a power of villainy walking the world, Martin Doul, among them that do be gadding around with their gaping eyes, and their sweet words, and they with no sense in them at all.

MARTIN DOUL — *sadly.*— It's the truth, maybe, and yet I'm told it's a grand thing to see a young girl walking the road.

MARY DOUL. You'd be as bad as the rest of them if you had your sight, and I did well, surely, not to marry a seeing man —

it's scores would have had me and welcome — for the seeing is a queer lot, and you'd never know the thing they'd do.

[*A moment's pause.*

MARTIN DOUL — *listening.* — There's some one coming on the road.

MARY DOUL. Let you put the pith away out of their sight, or they'll be picking it out with the spying eyes they have, and saying it's rich we are, and not sparing us a thing at all.

[*They bundle away the rushes. Timmy the smith comes in on left.*

MARTIN DOUL — *with a begging voice.* — Leave a bit of silver for blind Martin, your honour. Leave a bit of silver, or a penny copper itself, and we'll be praying the Lord to bless you and you going the way.

TIMMY — *stopping before them.* — And you letting on a while back you knew my step!

[*He sits down.*

MARTIN — *with his natural voice.* — I know it when Molly Bryne's walking in front, or when she's two perches, maybe, lagging behind; but it's few times I've heard you walking up the like of that, as if you'd met a thing wasn't right and you coming on the road.
the road.

TIMMY — *hot and breathless, wiping his face.*— You've good ears, God bless you, if you're a liar itself; for I'm after walking up in great haste from hearing wonders in the fair.

MARTIN DOUL — *rather contemptuously.*— You're always hearing queer wonderful things, and the lot of them nothing at all; but I'm thinking, this time, it's a strange thing surely you'd be walking up before the turn of day, and not waiting below to look on them lepping, or dancing, or playing shows on the green of Clash.

TIMMY — *huffed.*— I was coming to tell you it's in this place there'd be a bigger wonder done in a short while (*Martin Doul stops working*) than was ever done on the green of Clash, or the width of Leinster itself; but you're thinking, maybe, you're too cute a little fellow to be minding me at all.

MARTIN DOUL — *amused, but incredulous.*— There'll be wonders in this place, is it?

TIMMY. Here at the crossing of the roads.

MARTIN DOUL. I never heard tell of anything to happen in this place since the night they killed the old fellow going home with his gold, the Lord have mercy on him, and threw down his corpse into the bog. Let them not be doing the like of that this night, for it's ourselves have a right to the crossing roads, and we don't want any of your bad tricks, or your wonders either, for it's wonder enough we are ourselves.

TIMMY. If I'd a mind I'd be telling you of a real wonder this day, and the way you'll be having a great joy, maybe, you're not thinking on at all.

MARTIN DOUL — *interested.*— Are they putting up a still behind in the rocks? It'd be a grand thing if I'd sup handy the way I wouldn't be destroying myself groping up across the bogs in the rain falling.

TIMMY — *still moodily.*— It's not a still they're bringing, or the like of it either.

MARY DOUL — *persuasively, to Timmy.* — Maybe they're hanging a thief, above at the bit of a tree. I'm told it's a great sight to see a man hanging by his neck; but what joy would that be to ourselves, and we not seeing it at all?

TIMMY — *more pleasantly.*— They're hanging no one this day, Mary Doul, and yet, with the help of God, you'll see a power hanged before you die.

MARY DOUL. Well you've queer humbuging talk. . . . What way would I see a power hanged, and I a dark woman since the seventh year of my age?

TIMMY. Did ever you hear tell of a place across a bit of the sea, where there is an island, and the grave of the four beautiful saints?

MARY DOUL. I've heard people have walked round from the west and they speaking of that.

TIMMY — *impressively.*— There's a green ferny well, I'm told, behind of that place, and if you put a drop of the water out of it on the eyes of a blind man, you'll make him see as well as any person is walking the world.

MARTIN DOUL — *with excitement.*— Is that the truth, Timmy? I'm thinking you're telling a lie.

TIMMY — *gruffly.*— That's the truth, Martin Doul, and you may believe it now, for you're after believing a power of things weren't as likely at all.

MARY DOUL. Maybe we could send us a young lad to bring us the water. I could wash a naggin bottle in the morning, and I'm thinking Patch Ruadh would go for it, if we gave him a good drink, and the bit of money we have hid in the thatch.

TIMMY. It'd be no good to be sending a sinful man the like of ourselves, for I'm told the holiness of the water does be getting soiled with the villainy of your heart, the time you'd be carrying it, and you looking round on the girls, maybe, or drinking a small sup at a still.

MARTIN DOUL — *with disappointment.* —It'd be a long terrible way to be walking ourselves, and I'm thinking that's a wonder will bring small joy to us at all.

TIMMY — *turning on him impatiently.*— What is it you want with your walking? It's as deaf as blind you're growing if you're not after hearing me say it's in this place the wonder would be done.

MARTIN DOUL — *with a flash of anger.* — If it is can't you open the big slobbering mouth you have and say what way it'll be done, and not be making blather till the fall of night.

TIMMY — *jumping up.*— I'll be going on now (*Mary Doul rises*), and not wasting time talking civil talk with the like of you.

MARY DOUL — *standing up, disguising her impatience.*— Let you come here to me, Timmy, and not be minding him at all. (*Timmy stops, and she gropes up to him and takes him by the coat*). You're not huffy with myself, and let you tell me the whole story and don't be fooling me more. . . . Is it yourself has brought us the water?

TIMMY. It is not, surely.

MARY DOUL. Then tell us your wonder, Timmy. . . . What person'll bring it at all?

TIMMY — *relenting.*— It's a fine holy man will bring it, a saint of the Almighty God.

MARY DOUL — *overawed.*— A saint is it?

TIMMY. Ay, a fine saint, who's going round through the churches of Ireland, with a long cloak on him, and naked feet, for he's brought a sup of the water slung at his side, and, with the like of him, any little drop is enough to cure the dying, or to make the blind see as clear as the gray hawks do be high up, on a still day, sailing the sky.

MARTIN DOUL — *feeling for his stick.* —What place is he, Timmy? I'll be walking to him now.

TIMMY. Let you stay quiet, Martin. He's straying around saying prayers at the churches and high crosses, between this place and the hills, and he with a great crowd going behind — for it's fine prayers he does be saying, and fasting with it, till he's as thin as one of the empty rushes you have there on your knee; then he'll be coming after to this place to cure the two of you — we're after telling him the way you are — and to say his prayers in the church.

MARTIN DOUL — *turning suddenly to Mary Doul.*— And we'll be seeing ourselves this day. Oh, glory be to God, is it true surely?

MARY DOUL — *very pleased, to Timmy.* — Maybe I'd have time to walk down and get the big shawl I have below, for I do look my best, I've heard them say, when I'm dressed up with that thing on my head.

TIMMY. You'd have time surely ——

MARTIN DOUL — *listening.* — Whist now. . . I hear people again coming by the stream.

TIMMY — *looking out left, puzzled.*— It's the young girls I left walking after the Saint. . . . They're coming now (*goes up to entrance*) carrying things in their hands, and they walking as easy as you'd see a child walk who'd have a dozen eggs hid in her bib.

MARTIN DOUL — *listening.* — That's Molly Byrne, I'm thinking.

[*Molly Byrne and Bride come on left and cross to Martin Doul, carrying water-can, Saint's bell, and cloak.*

MOLLY — *volubly.*— God bless you, Martin. I've holy water here, from the grave of the four saints of the west, will have you cured in a short while and seeing like ourselves ——

TIMMY — *crosses to Molly, interrupting her.*— He's heard that. God help you. But where at all is the Saint, and what way is he after trusting the holy water with the likes of you?

MOLLY BYRNE. He was afeard to go a far way with the clouds is coming beyond, so he's gone up now through the thick woods to say a prayer at the crosses of Grianan, and he's coming on this road to the church.

TIMMY — *still astonished.*— And he's after leaving the holy water with the two of you? It's a wonder, surely.

[*Comes down left a little.*

MOLLY BYRNE. The lads told him no person could carry them things through the briars, and steep, slippy-feeling rocks he'll be climbing above, so he looked round then, and gave the water, and his big cloak, and his bell to the two of us, for young girls, says he, are the cleanest holy people you'd see walking the world.

[*Mary Doul goes near seat.*

MARY DOUL — *sits down, laughing to herself.*— Well, the Saint's a simple fellow, and it's no lie.

MARTIN DOUL — *leaning forward, holding out his hands.*— Let you give me the water in my hand, Molly Byrne, the way I'll know you have it surely.

MOLLY BYRNE — *giving it to him.*— Wonders is queer things, and maybe it'd cure you, and you holding it alone.

MARTIN DOUL — *looking round.*— It does not, Molly. I'm not seeing at all. (*He shakes the can.*) There's a small sup only. Well, isn't it a great wonder the little trifling thing would bring seeing to the blind, and be showing us the big women and the young girls, and all the fine things is walking the world.

[*He feels for Mary Doul and gives her the can.*

MARY DOUL — *shaking it.*— Well, glory be to God ——

MARTIN DOUL — *pointing to Bride.*— And what is it herself has, making sounds in her hand?

BRIDE — *crossing to Martin Doul.*— It's the Saint's bell; you'll hear him ringing out the time he'll be going up some place, to be saying his prayers.

[*Martin Doul holds out his hand; she gives it to him.*

MARTIN DOUL — *ringing it.*— It's a sweet, beautiful sound.

MARY DOUL. You'd know, I'm thinking, by the little silvery voice of it, a fasting holy man was after carrying it a great way at his side.

[*Bride crosses a little right behind Martin Doul.*

MOLLY BYRNE — *unfolding Saint's cloak.*— Let you stand up now, Martin Doul, till I put his big cloak on you. (*Martin Doul rises, comes forward, centre a little.*) The way we'd see how you'd look, and you a saint of the Almighty God.

MARTIN DOUL — *standing up, a little diffidently.*— I've heard the priests a power of times making great talk and praises of the beauty of the saints.

[*Molly Byrne slips cloak round him.*

TIMMY — *uneasily.*— You'd have a right to be leaving him alone, Molly. What would the Saint say if he seen you making game with his cloak?

MOLLY BYRNE — *recklessly.* — How would he see us, and he saying prayers in the wood? (*She turns Martin Doul round.*) Isn't that a fine, holy-looking saint, Timmy the smith? (*Laughing foolishly.*) There's a grand, handsome fellow, Mary Doul; and if you seen him now you'd be as proud, I'm thinking, as the archangels below, fell out with the Almighty God.

MARY DOUL — *with quiet confidence going to Martin Doul and feeling his cloak.* — It's proud we'll be this day, surely.

[*Martin Doul is still ringing.*

MOLLY BYRNE — *to Martin Doul.* — Would you think well to be all your life walking round the like of that, Martin Doul, and you bell-ringing with the saints of God?

MARY DOUL — *turning on her, fiercely.* — How would he be bell-ringing with the saints of God and he wedded with myself?

MARTIN DOUL. It's the truth she's saying, and if bell-ringing is a fine life, yet I'm thinking, maybe, it's better I am wedded with the beautiful dark woman of Ballinatone.

MOLLY BYRNE — *scornfully.* — You're thinking that, God help you; but it's little you know of her at all.

MARTIN DOUL. It's little surely, and

I'm destroyed this day waiting to look upon her face.

TIMMY — *awkwardly.*— It's well you know the way she is; for the like of you do have great knowledge in the feeling of your hands.

MARTIN DOUL — *still feeling the cloak.* — We do, maybe. Yet it's little I know of faces, or of fine beautiful cloaks, for it's few cloaks I've had my hand to, and few faces (*plaintively*); for the young girls is mighty shy, Timmy the smith, and it isn't much they heed me, though they do be saying I'm a handsome man.

MARY DOUL — *mockingly, with good humour.*— Isn't it a queer thing the voice he puts on him, when you hear him talking of the skinny-looking girls, and he married with a woman he's heard called the wonder of the western world?

TIMMY — *pityingly.*— The two of you will see a great wonder this day, and it's no lie.

MARTIN DOUL. I've heard tell her yellow hair, and her white skin, and her big eyes are a wonder, surely ——

BRIDE — *who has looked out left.*— Here's the Saint coming from the selvage of the wood. . . . Strip the cloak from him, Molly, or he'll be seeing it now.

MOLLY BYRNE — *hastily to Bride.*— Take the bell and put yourself by the stones. (*To Martin Doul.*) Will you hold your head up till I loosen the cloak? (*She pulls off the cloak and throws it over her arm. Then she pushes Martin Doul over and stands him beside Mary Doul.*) Stand there now, quiet, and let you not be saying a word.

[*She and Bride stand a little on their left, demurely, with bell, etc., in their hands.*

MARTIN DOUL — *nervously arranging his clothes.*— Will he mind the way we are, and not tidied or washed cleanly at all?

MOLLY BYRNE. He'll not see what way you are. . . . He'd walk by the finest woman in Ireland, I'm thinking, and not trouble to raise his two eyes to look upon her face. . . . Whisht!

[*The Saint comes left, with crowd.*

SAINT. Are these the two poor people?

TIMMY — *officiously.*— They are, holy father; they do be always sitting here at the crossing of the roads, asking a bit of copper from them that do pass, or stripping rushes for lights, and they not mournful at all, but talking out straight with a full voice, and making game with them that likes it.

SAINT — *to Martin Doul and Mary Doul.* — It's a hard life you've had not seeing sun or moon, or the holy priests itself praying to the Lord, but it's the like of you who are brave in a bad time will make a fine use of the gift of sight the Almighty God will bring to you today. (*He takes his cloak and puts it about him.*) It's on a bare starving rock that there's the grave of the four beauties of God, the way it's little wonder, I'm thinking, if it's with bare starving people the water should be used. (*He takes the water and bell and slings them round his shoulders.*) So it's to the like of yourselves I do be going, who are wrinkled and poor, a thing rich men would hardly look at at all, but would throw

MARTIN DOUL — *moving uneasily.*— When they look on herself, who is a fine woman ——

TIMMY — *shaking him.*— Whisht now, and be listening to the Saint.

SAINT — *looks at them a moment, continues.*— If it's raggy and dirty you are itself, I'm saying, the Almighty God isn't at all like the rich men of Ireland; and, with the power of the water I'm after bringing in a little curagh into Cashla Bay, He'll have pity on you, and put sight into your eyes.

MARTIN DOUL — *taking off his hat.*— I'm ready now, holy father ——

SAINT — *taking him by the hand.*— I'll cure you first, and then I'll come for your wife. We'll go up now into the church, for I must say a prayer to the Lord. (*To Mary Doul, as he moves off.*) And let you be making your mind still and saying praises in your heart, for it's a great wonderful thing when the power of the Lord of the world is brought down upon your like.

PEOPLE — *pressing after him.*— Come now till we watch.

BRIDE. Come, Timmy.

SAINT — *waving them back.*— Stay back where you are, for I'm not wanting a big crowd making whispers in the church. Stay back there, I'm saying, and you'd do well to be thinking on the way sin has brought blindness to the world, and to be saying a prayer for your own sakes against false prophets and heathens, and the words of women and smiths, and all knowledge that would soil the soul or the body of a man.

[*People shrink back. He goes into church. Mary Doul gropes half-way towards the door and kneels near path. People form a group at right.*

TIMMY. Isn't it a fine, beautiful voice he has, and he a fine, brave man if it wasn't for the fasting?

BRIDE Did you watch his moving his hands?

MOLLY BYRNE. It'd be a fine thing if some one in this place could pray the like of him, for I'm thinking the water from our own blessed well would do rightly if a man knew the way to be saying prayers, and then there'd be no call to be bringing water from that wild place, where, I'm told, there are no decent houses, or fine-looking people at all.

BRIDE — *who is looking in at door from right.*— Look at the great trembling Martin has shaking him, and he on his knees.

TIMMY — *anxiously.*— God help him. . . What will he be doing when he sees his wife this day? I'm thinking it was bad work we did when we let on she was fine-looking, and not a wrinkled, wizened hag the way she is.

MAT SIMON. Why would he be vexed, and we after giving him great joy and pride, the time he was dark?

MOLLY BYRNE — *sitting down in Mary Doul's seat and tidying her hair.*— If it's vexed he is itself, he'll have other things now to think on as well as his wife; and what does any man care for a wife, when it's two weeks or three, he is looking on her face?

MAT SIMON. That's the truth now, Molly, and it's more joy dark Martin got from the lies we told of that hag is kneeling by the path than your own man will get from you, day or night, and he living at your side.

MOLLY BYRNE — *defiantly.*— Let you not be talking, Mat Simon, for it's not yourself will be my man, though you'd be crowing and singing fine songs if you'd that hope in you at all.

TIMMY — *shocked, to Molly Byrne.*— Let you not be raising your voice when the Saint's above at his prayers.

BRIDE — *crying out.*— Whisht. . . . Whisht. . . . I'm thinking he's cured.

MARTIN DOUL — *crying out in the church.*— Oh, glory be to God. . . .

SAINT — *solemnly.*— Laus patri sit et
filio cum spiritu paraclito
Qui suae dono gratiae misertus est Hiberniae. . . .

MARTIN DOUL—*estatically.*—Oh, glory be to God, I see now surely. . . . I see the walls of the church, and the green bits of ferns in them, and yourself, holy father, and the great width of the sky.

[*He runs out half-foolish with joy, and comes past Mary Doul as she scrambles to her feet, drawing a little away from her at he goes by.*

TIMMY — *to the others.*— He doesn't know her at all.

The Saint comes out behind Martin Doul, and leads Mary Doul into the church. Martin Doul comes on to the People. The men are between him and the Girls; he verifies his position with his stick.

MARTIN DOUL — *crying out joyfully.*— That's Timmy, I know Timmy by the black of his head. . . . That's Mat Simon, I know Mat by the length of his legs. . . . That should be Patch Ruadh, with the gamey eyes in him, and the fiery hair. (*He sees Molly Byrne on Mary Doul's seat, and his voice changes completely.*) Oh, it was no lie they told me, Mary Doul. Oh, glory to God and the seven saints I didn't die and not see you at all. The blessing of God on the water, and the feet carried it round through the land. The blessing of God on this day, and them that brought me the Saint, for it's grand hair you have (*she lowers her head a little confused*), and soft skin, and eyes would make the saints, if they were dark awhile and seeing again, fall down out of the sky. (*He goes nearer to her.*) Hold up your head, Mary, the way I'll see it's richer I am than the great kings of the east. Hold up your head, I'm saying, for it's soon you'll be seeing me, and I not a bad one at all.

[*He touches her and she starts up.*

MOLLY BYRNE. Let you keep away from me, and not be soiling my chin.

[*People laugh heartily.*

MARTIN DOUL—*bewildered.*—It's Molly's voice you have.

MOLLY BYRNE. Why wouldn't I have my own voice? Do you think I'm a ghost?

MARTIN DOUL. Which of you all is herself? (*He goes up to Bride.*) Is it you is Mary Doul? I'm thinking you're more the like of what they said (*peering at her.*) For you've yellow hair, and white skin, and it's the smell of my own turf is rising from your shawl.

[*He catches her shawl.*

BRIDE—*pulling away her shawl.*—I'm not your wife, and let you get out of my way.

[*The People laugh again.*

MARTIN DOUL — *with misgiving, to another Girl.*— Is it yourself it is? You're not so fine-looking, but I'm thinking you'd do, with the grand nose you have, and your nice hands and your feet.

GIRL — *scornfully.*— I never seen any person that took me for blind, and a seeing woman, I'm thinking, would never wed the like of you.

[*She turns away, and the People laugh once more, drawing back a little and leaving him on their left.*

PEOPLE — *jeeringly.*— Try again, Martin, try again, and you'll be finding her yet.

MARTIN DOUL — *passionately.*—Where is it you have her hidden away? Isn't it a black shame for a drove of pitiful beasts the like of you to be making game of me, and putting a fool's head on me the grand day of my life? Ah, you're thinking you're a fine lot, with your giggling, weeping eyes, a fine lot to be making game of myself and the woman I've heard called the great wonder of the west.

[*During this speech, which he gives with his back towards the church, Mary Doul has come out with her sight cured, and come down towards the right with a silly simpering smile, till she is a little behind Martin Doul.*

MARY DOUL—*when he pauses.*—Which of you is Martin Doul?

MARTIN DOUL—*wheeling round.*—It's her voice surely.

[*They stare at each other blankly.*

MOLLY BYRNE—*to Martin Doul.*—Go up now and take her under the chin and be speaking the way you spoke to myself.

MARTIN DOUL—*in a low voice, with intensity.*—If I speak now, I'll speak hard to the two of you——

MOLLY BYRNE—*to Mary Doul.*—You're not saying a word, Mary. What is it you think of himself, with the fat legs on him, and the little neck like a ram?

MARY DOUL. I'm thinking it's a poor thing when the Lord God gives you sight and puts the like of that man in your way.

MARTIN DOUL. It's on your two knees you should be thanking the Lord God you're not looking on yourself, for if it was yourself you seen you'd be running round in a short while like the old screeching mad-woman is running round in the glen.

MARY DOUL—*beginning to realize her-*

self.— If I'm not so fine as some of them said, skin ——

MARTIN DOUL — *breaking out into a passionate cry.*— Your hair, and your big eyes, is it? . . . I'm telling you there isn't a wisp on any gray mare on the ridge of the world isn't finer than the dirty twist on your head. There isn't two eyes in any starving sow isn't finer than the eyes you were calling blue like the sea.

MARY DOUL — *interrupting him.*— It's the devil cured you this day with your talking of sows; it's the devil cured you this day, I'm saying, and drove you crazy with lies.

MARTIN DOUL. Isn't it yourself is after playing lies on me, ten years, in the day and in the night; but what is that to you now the Lord God has given eyes to me, the way I see you an old wizendy hag, was never fit to rear a child to me itself.

MARY DOUL. I wouldn't rear a crumpled whelp the like of you. It's many a woman is married with finer than yourself should be praising God if she's no child, and isn't loading the earth with things would make the heavens lonesome above, and they scaring the larks, and the crows, and the angels passing in the sky.

MARTIN DOUL. Go on now to be seeking a lonesome place where the earth can hide you away; go on now, I'm saying, or you'll be having men and women with their knees bled, and they screaming to God for a holy water would darken their sight, for there's no man but would liefer be blind a hundred years, or a thousand itself, than to be looking on your like.

MARY DOUL — *raising her stick.*—Maybe if I hit you a strong blow you'd be blind again, and having what you want ——

The Saint is seen in the church door with his head bent in prayer.

MARTIN DOUL — *raising his stick and driving Mary Doul back towards left.*— Let you keep off from me now if you wouldn't have me strike out the little handful of brains you have about on the road.

[*He is going to strike her, but Timmy catches him by the arm.*

TIMMY. Have you no shame to be making a great row, and the Saint above saying his prayers?

MARTIN DOUL. What is it I care for the like of him? (*Struggling to free himself*). Let me hit her one good one, for the love of the Almighty God, and I'll be quiet after till I die.

TIMMY—*shaking him.*—Will you whisht, I'm saying.

SAINT—*coming forward, centre.*—Are their minds troubled with joy, or is their sight uncertain, the way it does often be the day a person is restored?

TIMMY. It's too certain their sight is, holy father; and they're after making a great fight, because they're a pair of pitiful shows.

SAINT—*coming between them.*—May the Lord who has given you sight send a little sense into your heads, the way it won't be on your two selves you'll be looking—on two pitiful sinners of the earth—but on the splendour of the Spirit of God, you'll see an odd time shining out through the big hills, and steep streams falling to the sea. For if it's on the like of that you do be thinking, you'll not be minding the faces of men, but you'll be saying prayers and great praises, till you'll be living the way the great saints do be living, with little but old sacks, and skin covering their bones. (*To Timmy.*) Leave him go now, you're seeing he's quiet again. (*He frees Martin Doul.*) And let you (*he turns to Mary Doul*) not be raising your voice, a bad thing in a woman; but let the lot of you, who have seen the power of the Lord, be thinking on it in the dark night, and be saying to yourselves it's great pity and love He has for the poor, starving people of Ireland. (*He gathers his cloak about him.*) And now the Lord send blessing to you all, for I am going on to Annagolan, where there is a deaf woman, and to Laragh, where there are two men without sense, and to Glenassil, where there are children blind from their birth; and then I'm going to sleep this night in the bed of the holy Kevin, and to be praising God, and asking great blessing on you all.

[*He bends his head.*

CURTAIN

ACT II

Village roadside, on left the door of a forge, with broken wheels, etc., lying about. A well near centre, with board above it, and room to pass behind it. Martin Doul is sitting near forge, cutting sticks.

TIMMY — *heard hammering inside forge, then calls.*— Let you make haste out there. . . . I'll be putting up new fires at the turn of day, and you haven't the half of them cut yet.

MARTIN DOUL — *gloomily.*— It's destroyed I'll be whacking your old thorns till the turn of day, and I with no food in my stomach would keep the life in a pig. (*He turns towards the door.*) Let you come out here and cut them yourself if you want them cut, for there's an hour every day when a man has a right to his rest.

TIMMY — *coming out, with a hammer, impatiently.*— Do you want me to be driving you off again to be walking the roads? There you are now, and I giving you your food, and a corner to sleep, and money with it; and, to hear the talk of you, you'd think I was after beating you, or stealing your gold.

MARTIN DOUL. You'd do it handy, maybe, if I'd gold to steal.

TIMMY — *throws down hammer; picks up some of the sticks already cut, and throws them into door.*) There's no fear of your having gold — a lazy, basking fool the like of you.

MARTIN DOUL. No fear, maybe, and I here with yourself, for it's more I got a while since, and I sitting blinded in Grianan, than I get in this place working hard, and destroying myself, the length of the day.

TIMMY — *stopping with amazement.*— Working hard? (*He goes over to him.*) I'll teach you to work hard, Martin Doul. Strip off your coat now, and put a tuck in your sleeves, and cut the lot of them, while I'd rake the ashes from the forge, or I'll not put up with you another hour itself.

MARTIN DOUL — *horrified.* — Would you have me getting my death sitting out in the black wintry air with no coat on me at all?

TIMMY — *with authority.*— Strip it off now, or walk down upon the road.

MARTIN DOUL — *bitterly.*— Oh, God help me! (*He begins taking off his coat.*) I've heard tell you stripped the sheet from your wife and you putting her down into the grave, and that there isn't the like of you for plucking your living ducks, the short days, and leaving them running round in their skins, in the great rains and the cold. (*He tucks up his sleeves.*) Ah, I've heard a power of queer things of yourself, and there isn't one of them I'll not believe from this day, and be telling to the boys.

TIMMY — *pulling over a big stick.*— Let you cut that now, and give me rest from your talk, for I'm not heeding you at all.

MARTIN DOUL — *taking stick.*— That's a hard, terrible stick, Timmy; and isn't it a poor thing to be cutting strong timber the like of that, when it's cold the bark is, and slippy with the frost of the air?

TIMMY — *gathering up another armful of sticks.*— What way wouldn't it be cold, and it freezing since the moon was changed?

[*He goes into forge.*

MARTIN DOUL — *querulously, as he cuts slowly.*— What way, indeed, Timmy? For it's a raw, beastly day we do have each day, till I do be thinking it's well for the blind don't be seeing them gray clouds driving on the hill, and don't be looking on people with their noses red, the like of your nose, and their eyes weeping and watering, the like of your eyes, God help you, Timmy the smith.

TIMMY — *seen blinking in doorway.*— Is it turning now you are against your sight.

MARTIN DOUL — *very miserably.*— It's a hard thing for a man to have his sight, and he living near to the like of you (*he cuts a stick and throws it away*), or wed with a wife (*cuts a stick*); and I do be thinking it should be a hard thing for the Almighty God to be looking on the world, bad days, and on men the like of yourself walking around on it, and they slipping each way in the muck.

TIMMMY — *with pot-hooks which he taps on anvil.*— You'd have a right to be minding, Martin Doul, for it's a power the Saint cured lose their sight after a while. Mary Doul's dimming again, I've heard them say; and I'm thinking the Lord, if he hears you making that talk, will have little pity left for you at all.

MARTIN DOUL. There's not a bit of fear of me losing my sight, and if it's a dark day itself it's too well I see every wicked wrinkle you have round by your eye.

TIMMY — *looking at him sharply.*— The day's not dark since the clouds broke in the east.

MARTIN DOUL. Let you not be tormenting yourself trying to make me afeard. You told me a power of bad lies the time I was blind, and it's right now for you to stop, and be taking your rest (*Mary Doul comes in unnoticed on right with a sack filled with green stuff on her arm*), for it's little ease or quiet any person would get if the big fools of Ireland were't weary at times. (*He looks up and sees Mary Doul.*) Oh. glory be to God, she's coming again.

[*He begins to work busily with his back to her.*

TIMMY — *amused, to Mary Doul, as she is going by without looking at them.*— Look on him now, Mary Doul. You'd be a great one for keeping him steady at his work, for he's after idling and blathering to this hour from the dawn of day.

MARY DOUL — *stiffly.*— Of what is it you're speaking, Timmy the smith?

TIMMY — *laughing.*— Of himself, surely. Look on him there, and he with the shirt on him ripping from his back. You'd have a right to come round this night, I'm thinking, and put a stitch into his clothes, for it's long enough you are not speaking one to the other.

MARY DOUL. Let the two of you not torment me at all.

[*She goes out left, with her head in the air.*

MARTIN DOUL—*stops work and looks after her.*—Well, isn't it a queer thing she can't keep herself two days without looking on my face?

TIMMY—*jeeringly.*—Looking on your face is it? And she after going by with her head turned the way you'd see a priest going where there'd be a drunken man in the side ditch talking with a girl. (*Martin Doul gets up and goes to corner of forge, and looks out left.*) Come back here and don't mind her at all. Come back here, I'm saying, you've no call to be spying behind her since she went off, and left you, in place of breaking her heart, trying to keep you in the decency of clothes and food.

MARTIN DOUL—*crying out indignantly.*—You know rightly, Timmy, it was myself drove her away.

TIMMY. That's a lie you're telling, yet it's little I care which one of you was driving the other, and let you walk back here, I'm saying, to your work.

MARTIN DOUL — *turning round.*— I'm coming, surely.

[*He stops and looks out right, going a step or two towards centre.*

TIMMY. On what is it you're gaping, Martin Doul?

MARTIN DOUL. There's a person walking above. . . . It's Molly Byrne, I'm thinking, coming down with her can.

TIMMY. If she is itself let you not be idling this day, or minding her at all, and let you hurry with them sticks, for I'll want you in a short while to be blowing in the forge.

[*He throws down pot-hooks.*

MARTIN DOUL — *crying out.*— Is it roasting me now you'd be? (*Turns back and sees pot-hooks; he takes them up.*) Pot-hooks? Is it over them you've been inside sneezing and sweating since the dawn of day?

TIMMY — *resting himself on anvil, with satisfaction.*) I'm making a power of things you do have when you're settling with a wife, Martin Doul; for I heard tell last night the Saint'll be passing again in a short while, and I'd have him wed Molly with myself. . . . He'd do it, I've heard them say, for not a penny at all.

MARTIN DOUL — *lays down hooks and*

looks at him steadily.— Molly'll be saying great praises now to the Almighty God and He giving her a fine, stout, hardy man the like of you.

TIMMY — *uneasily.*— And why wouldn't she, if she's a fine woman itself?

MARTIN DOUL — *looking up right.*— Why wouldn't she, indeed, Timmy? .... The Almighty God's made a fine match in the two of you, for if you went marrying a woman was the like of yourself you'd be having the fearfullest little children, I'm thinking, was ever seen in the world.

TIMMY — *seriously offended.*— God forgive you! if you're an ugly man to be looking at, I'm thinking your tongue's worse than your view.

MARTIN DOUL — *hurt also.*— Isn't it destroyed with the cold I am, and if I'm ugly itself I never seen anyone the like of you for dreepiness this day, Timmy the smith, and I'm thinking now herself's coming above you'd have a right to step up into your old shanty, and give a rub to your face, and not be sitting there with your bleary eyes, and your big nose, the like of an old scarecrow stuck down upon the road.

TIMMY — *looking up the road uneasily.*—

She's no call to mind what way I look, and I after building a house with four rooms in it above on the hill. (*He stands up.*) But it's a queer thing the way yourself and Mary Doul are after setting every person in this place, and up beyond to Rathvanna, talking of nothing, and thinking of nothing, but the way they do be looking in the face. (*Going towards forge.*) It's the devil's work you're after doing with your talk of fine looks, and I'd do right, maybe, to step in and wash the blackness from my eyes.

[*He goes into forge. Martin Doul rubs his face furtively with the tail of his coat. Molly Byrne comes on right with a water-can, and begins to fill it at the well.*

MARTIN DOUL. God save you, Molly Byrne.

MOLLY BYRNE — *indifferently.*— God save you.

MARTIN DOUL. That's a dark, gloomy day, and the Lord have mercy on us all.

MOLLY BYRNE. Middling dark.

MARTIN DOUL. It's a power of dirty days, and dark mornings, and shabby-looking fellows (*he makes a gesture over his shoulder*) we do have to be looking on when we have our sight, God help us, but there's one fine thing we have, to be looking on a grand, white, handsome girl, the like of you . . . . and every time I set my eyes on you I do be blessing the saints, and the holy water, and the power of the Lord Almighty in the heavens above.

MOLLY BYRNE. I've heard the priests say it isn't looking on a young girl would teach many to be saying their prayers.

[*Bailing water into her can with a cup.*

MARTIN DOUL. It isn't many have been the way I was, hearing your voice speaking, and not seeing you at all.

MOLLY BYRNE. That should have been a queer time for an old, wicked, coaxing fool to be sitting there with your eyes shut, and not seeing a sight of girl or woman passing the road.

MARTIN DOUL. It it was a queer time itself it was great joy and pride I had the time I'd hear your voice speaking and you passing to Grianan (*beginning to speak with plaintive intensity*), for it's of many a fine thing your voice would put a poor dark fellow in mind, and the day I'd hear it it's of little else at all I would be thinking.

MOLLY BYRNE. I'll tell your wife if you talk to me the like of that. . . . You've heard, maybe, she's below picking nettles for the widow O'Flinn, who took great pity on her when she seen the two of you fighting, and yourself putting shame on her at the crossing of the roads.

MARTIN DOUL — *impatiently.* — Is there no living person can speak a score of words to me, or say "God speed you," itself, without putting me in mind of the old woman, or that day either at Grianan?

MOLLY BYRNE — *maliciously.*— I was thinking it should be a fine thing to put you in mind of the day you called the grand day of your life.

MARTIN DOUL. Grand day, is it? (*Plaintively again, throwing aside his work, and leaning towards her.*) Or a bad black day when I was roused up and found I was the like of the little children do be listening to the stories of an old woman, and do be dreaming after in the dark night that it's in grand houses of gold they are, with speckled horses to ride, and do be waking again, in a short while, and they destroyed with the cold, and the thatch dripping, maybe, and the starved ass braying in the yard?

MOLLY BYRNE — *working indifferently.*— You've great romancing this day, Martin Doul. Was it up at the still you were at the fall of night?

MARTIN DOUL — *stands up, comes towards her, but stands at far (right) side of well.*— It was not, Molly Byrne, but lying down in a little rickety shed. . . . Lying down across a sop of straw, and I thinking I was seeing you walk, and hearing the sound of your step on a dry road, and hearing you again, and you laughing and making great talk in a high room with dry timber lining the roof. For it's a fine sound your voice has that time, and it's better I am, I'm thinking, lying down, the way a blind man does be lying, than to be sitting here in the gray light taking hard words of Timmy the smith.

MOLLY BYRNE — *looking at him with interest*). It's queer talk you have if it's a little, old, shabby stump of a man you are itself.

MARTIN DOUL. I'm not so old as you do hear them say.

MOLLY BYRNE. You're old, I'm thinking, to be talking that talk with a girl.

MARTIN DOUL — *despondingly.*— It's not a lie you're telling, maybe, for it's long years I'm after losing from the world, feeling love and talking love, with the old woman, and I fooled the whole while with the lies of Timmy the smith.

MOLLY BYRNE — *half invitingly.*—It's a fine way you're wanting to pay Timmy the smith. . . . And it's not his *lies* you're making love to this day, Martin Doul.

MARTIN DOUL. It is not, Molly, and the Lord forgive us all. (*He passes behind her and comes near her left.*) For I've heard tell there are lands beyond in Cahir Iveraghig and the Reeks of Cork with warm sun in them, and fine light in the sky. (*Bending towards her.*) And light's a grand thing for a man ever was blind, or a woman, with a fine neck, and a skin on her the like of you, the way we'd have a right to go off this day till we'd have a fine life passing abroad through them towns of the south, and we telling stories, maybe, or singing songs at the fairs.

MOLLY BYRNE — *turning round half amused, and looking him over from head to foot.*— Well, isn't it a queer thing when your own wife's after leaving you because you're a pitiful show, you'd talk the like of that to me?

MARTIN DOUL — *drawing back a little, hurt, but indignant.*— It's a queer thing, maybe, for all things is queer in the world. (*In a low voice with peculiar emphasis.*) But there's one thing I'm telling you, if she walked off away from me, it wasn't because of seeing me, and I no more than I am, but because I was looking on her with my two eyes, and she getting up, and eating her food, and combing her hair, and lying down for her sleep.

MOLLY BYRNE — *interested, off her guard.*— Wouldn't any married man you'd have be doing the like of that?

MARTIN DOUL — *seizing the moment that he has her attention.*— I'm thinking by the mercy of God it's few sees anything but them is blind for a space (*with excitement.*) It's a few sees the old woman rotting for the grave, and it's few sees the like of yourself. (*He bends over her.*) Though it's shining you are, like a high lamp would drag in the ships out of the sea.

MOLLY BYRNE — *shrinking away from him.*— Keep off from me, Martin Doul.

MARTIN DOUL — *quickly, with low, furious intensity.*— It's the truth I'm telling you. (*He puts his hand on her shoulder and shakes her.*) And you'd do right not to marry a man is after looking out a long while on the bad days of the world; for what way would the like of him have fit eyes to look on yourself, when you rise up in the morning and come out of the little door you have above in the lane, the time it'd be a fine thing if a man would be seeing, and losing his sight, the way he'd have your two eyes facing him, and he going the roads, and shining above him, and he looking in the sky, and springing up from the earth, the time he'd lower his head, in place of the muck that seeing men do meet all roads spread on the world.

MOLLY BYRNE — *who has listened half mesmerized, starting away*). It's the like of that talk you'd hear from a man would be losing his mind.

MARTIN DOUL — *going after her, passing to her right.*— It'd be little wonder if a man near the like of you would be losing his mind. Put down your can now, and come along with myself, for I'm seeing you this day, seeing you, maybe, the way no man has seen you in the world. (*He takes her by the arm and trys to pull her away softly to the right.*) Let you come on now, I'm saying, to the lands of Iveragh and the Reeks of Cork, where you won't set down the width of your two feet and not be crushing fine flowers, and making sweet smells in the air.

MOLLY BYRNE — *laying down the can; trying to free herself.*— Leave me go, Martin Doul! Leave me go, I'm saying!

MARTIN DOUL. Let you not be fooling. Come along now the little path through the trees.

MOLLY BYRNE — *crying out towards forge.*— Timmy — Timmy the smith (*Timmy comes out of forge, and Martin Doul lets her go. Molly Byrne, excited and breathless, pointing to Martin Doul.*) Did ever you hear that them that loses their sight loses their senses along with it, Timmy the smith!

TIMMY — *suspicious, but uncertain.* — He's no sense, surely, and he'll be having himself driven off this day from where he's good sleeping, and feeding, and wages for his work.

MOLLY BYRNE — *as before.*— He's a bigger fool than that, Timmy. Look on him now, and tell me if that isn't a grand fellow to think he's only to open his mouth to have a fine woman, the like of me, running along by his heels.

[*Martin Doul recoils towards centre, with his hand to his eyes; Mary Doul is seen on left coming forward softly.*

TIMMY — *with blank amazement.*— Oh, the blind is wicked people, and it's no lie. But he'll walk off this day and not be troubling us more.

[*Turns back left and picks up Martin Doul's coat and stick; some things fall out of coat pocket, which he gathers up again.*

MARTIN DOUL — *turns round, sees Mary Doul, whispers to Molly Byrne with imploring agony.*— Let you not put shame on me, Molly, before herself and the smith. Let you not put shame on me and I after saying fine words to you, and dreaming . . . dreams . . . . in the night. (*He hesitates, and looks round the sky.*) Is it a storm of thunder is coming, or the last end of the world? (*He staggers towards Mary Doul, tripping slightly over tin can.*) The heavens is closing, I'm thinking, with darkness and great trouble passing in the sky. (*He reaches Mary Doul, and seizes her left arm with both his hands — with a frantic cry.*) Is it darkness of thunder is coming, Mary Doul! Do you see me clearly with your eyes?

MARY DOUL — *snatches her arm away, and hits him with empty sack across the face.*

— I see you a sight too clearly, and let you keep off from me now.

MOLLY BYRNE — *clapping her hands.* — That's right, Mary. That's the way to treat the like of him is after standing there at my feet and asking me to go off with him, till I'd grow an old wretched road-woman the like of yourself.

MARY DOUL — *defiantly.* — When the skin shrinks on your chin, Molly Byrne, there won't be the like of you for a shrunk hag in the four quarters of Ireland. . . . It's a fine pair you'd be, surely!

[*Martin Doul is standing at back right centre, with his back to the audience.*

TIMMY — *coming over to Mary Doul.* — Is it no shame you have to let on she'd ever be the like of you?

MARY DOUL. It's them that's fat and flabby do be wrinkled young, and that whitish yellowy hair she has does be soon turning the like of a handful of thin grass you'd see rotting, where the wet lies, at the north of a sty. (*Turning to go out on right.*) Ah, it's a better thing to have a simple, seemly face, the like of my face, for two-score years, or fifty itself, than to be setting fools mad a short while, and then to be turning a thing would drive off the little children from your feet.

[*She goes out; Martin Doul has come forward again, mastering himself, but uncertain.*

TIMMY. Oh, God protect us, Molly, from the words of the blind. (*He throws down Martin Doul's coat aad stick.*) There's your old rubbish now, Martin Doul, and let you take it up, for it's all you have, and walk off through the world, for if ever I meet you coming again, if it's seeing or blind you are itself, I'll bring out the big hammer and hit you a welt with it will leave you easy till the judgment day.

MARTIN DOUL — *rousing himself with an effort.*— What call have you to talk the like of that with myself?

TIMMY — *pointing to Molly Byrne.*— It's well you know what call I have. It's well you know a decent girl, I'm thinking to wed, has no right to have her heart scalded with hearing talk — and queer, bad talk, I'm thinking — from a raggy-looking fool the like of you.

MARTIN DOUL — *raising his voice.*— It's making game of you she is, for what seeing girl would marry with yourself? Look on him, Molly, look on him, I'm saying, for I'm seeing him still, and let you raise your voice, for the time is come, and bid him go up into his forge, and be sitting there by himself, sneezing and sweating, and he beating pot-hooks till the judgment day.

[*He seizes her arm again.*

MOLLY BYRNE. Keep him off from me, Timmy!

TIMMY — *pushing Martin Doul aside.*— Would you have me strike you, Martin Doul? Go along now after your wife, who's a fit match for you, and leave Molly with myself.

MARTIN DOUL — *despairingly.*— Won't you raise your voice, Molly, and lay hell's long curse on his tongue?

MOLLY BYRNE — *on Timmy's left.*— I'll be telling him it's destroyed I am with the sight of you and the sound of your voice. Go off now after your wife, and if she beats you again, let you go after the tinker girls is above running the hills, or down among the sluts of the town, and you'll learn one day, maybe, the way a man should speak with a well-reared, civil girl the like of me. (*She takes Timmy by the arm.*) Come up now into the forge till he'll be gone down a bit on the road, for it's near afeard I am of the wild look he has come in his eyes.

[*She goes into the forge. Timmy stops in the doorway.*

TIMMY. Let me not find you out here again, Martin Doul. (*He bares his arm.*) It's well you know Timmy the smith has great strength in his arm, and it's a power of things it has broken a sight harder than the old bone of your skull.

[*He goes into the forge and pulls the door after him.*

MARTIN DOUL — *stands a moment with his hand to his eyes.*— And that's the last thing I'm to set my sight on in the life of the world — the villainy of a woman and the bloody strength of a man. Oh, God, pity a poor, blind fellow, the way I am this day with no strength in me to do hurt to them at all. (*He begins groping about for a moment, then stops.*) Yet if I've no strength in me I've a voice left for my prayers, and may God blight them this day, and my own soul the same hour with them, the way I'll see them after, Molly Byrne and Timmy the smith, the two of them on a high bed, and they screeching in hell. . . . It'll be a grand thing that time to look on the two of them; and they twisting and roaring out, and twisting and roaring again, one day and the next day, and and each day always and ever. It's not blind I'll be that time, and it won't be hell to me, I'm thinking, but the like of heaven itself; and it's fine care I'll be taking the Lord Almighty doesn't know.

[*He turns to grope out.*

CURTAIN

ACT III

The same Scene as in first Act, but gap in centre has been filled with briars, or branches of some sort. Mary Doul, blind again, gropes her way in on left, and sits as before. She has a few rushes with her. It is an early spring day.

MARY DOUL — *mournfully.*— Ah, God help me . . . God help me; the blackness wasn't so black at all the other time as it is this time, and it's destroyed I'll be now, and hard set to get my living working alone, when it's few are passing and the winds are cold. (*She begins shredding rushes.*) I'm thinking short days will be long days to me from this time, and I sitting here, not seeing a blink, or hearing a word, and no thought in my mind but long prayers that Martin Doul'll get his reward in a short while for the villainy of his heart. It's great jokes the people'll be making now, I'm thinking, and they pass me by, pointing their fingers maybe, and asking what place is himself, the way it's no quiet or decency I'll have from this day till I'm an old woman with long white hair and it twisting from my brow. (*She fumbles with her hair, and then seems to hear something. Listens for a moment.*) There's a queer, slouching step coming on the road. . . . God help me, he's coming surely.

[*She stays perfectly quiet. Martin Doul gropes in on right, blind also.*

MARTIN DOUL — *gloomily.*— The devil mend Mary Doul for putting lies on me, and letting on she was grand. The devil mend the old Saint for letting me see it was lies. (*He sits down near her.*) The devil mend Timmy the smith for killing me with hard work, and keeping me with an empty, windy stomach in me, in the day and in the night. Ten thousand devils mend the soul of Molly Byrne — (*Mary Doul nods her head with approval*) — and the bad, wicked souls is hidden in all the women of the world. (*He rocks himself, with his hand over his face.*) It's lonesome I'll be from this day, and if living people is a bad lot, yet Mary Doul, herself, and she a dirty, wrinkled-looking hag, was better maybe to be sitting along with than no one at all. I'll be getting my death now, I'm thinking, sitting alone in the cold air, hearing the night coming, and the blackbirds flying round in the briars crying to themselves, the time you'll hear one cart getting off a long way in the east, and another cart getting off a long way in the west, and a dog barking maybe, and a little wind turning the sticks. (*He listens and sighs heavily.*) I'll be destroyed sitting alone and losing my senses this time the way I'm after losing my sight, for it'd make any person afeard to be sitting up hearing the sound of his breath — (*he moves his feet on the stones*) — and the noise of his feet, when it's a power of queer things do be stirring, little sticks breaking, and the grass moving — (*Mary Doul half sighs, and he turns on her in horror*) — till you'd take your dying oath on sun and moon a thing was breathing on the stones. (*He listens towards her for a moment, then starts up nervously, and gropes about for his stick.*) I'll be going now, I'm thinking, but I'm not sure what place my stick's in, and I'm destroyed with terror and dread. (*He touches her face as he is groping about and cries out.*) There's a thing with a cold, living face on it sitting up at my side. (*He turns to run away, but misses his path and stumbles in against the wall.*) My road is lost on me now! Oh, merciful God, set my foot on the path this day, and I'll be saying prayers morning and night, and not straining my ear after young girls, or doing any bad thing till I die——

MARY DOUL—*indignantly.*—Let you not be telling lies to the Almighty God.

MARTIN DOUL. Mary Doul, is it? (*Recovering himself with immense relief.*) Is it Mary Doul, I'm saying?

MARY DOUL. There's a sweet tone in your voice I've not heard for a space. You're taking me for Molly Byrne, I'm thinking.

MARTIN DOUL—*coming towards her, wiping sweat from his face.*—Well, sight's a queer thing for upsetting a man. It's a queer thing to think I'd live to this day to be fearing the like of you; but if it's shaken I am for a short while, I'll soon be coming to myself.

MARY DOUL. You'll be grand then, and it's no lie.

MARTIN DOUL—*sitting down shyly, some way off.*) You've no call to be talking, for I've heard tell you're as blind as myself.

MARY DOUL. If I am I'm bearing in mind I'm married to a little dark stump of a fellow looks the fool of the world, and I'll be bearing in mind from this day the great hullabuloo he's after making from hearing a poor woman breathing quiet in her place.

MARTIN DOUL. And you'll be bearing in mind, I'm thinking, what you seen a while back when you looked down into a well, or a clear pool, maybe, when there was no wind stirring and a good light in the sky.

MARY DOUL. I'm minding that surely, for if I'm not the way the liars were saying below I seen a thing in them pools put joy and blessing in my heart.

[*She puts her hand to her hair again.*

MARTIN DOUL — *laughing ironically.*— Well, they were saying below I was losing my senses, but I never went any day the length of that. . . . God help you, Mary Doul, if you're not a wonder for looks, you're the maddest female woman is walking the counties of the east.

MARY DOUL — *scornfully.*— You were saying all times you'd a great ear for hearing the lies of the world. A great ear, God help you, and you think you're using it now.

MARTIN DOUL. If it's not lies you're telling would you have me think you're not a wrinkled poor woman is looking like three scores, or two scores and a half!

MARY DOUL. I would not, Martin. (*She leans forward earnestly.*) For when I seen myself in them pools, I seen my hair would be gray or white, maybe, in a short while, and I seen with it that I'd a face would be a great wonder when it'll have soft white hair falling around it, the way when I'm an old woman there won't be the like of me surely in the seven counties of the east.

MARTIN DOUL — *with real admiration.* — You're a cute thinking woman, Mary Doul, and it's no lie.

MARY DOUL — *triumphantly.*— I am, surely, and I'm telling you a beautiful white-haired woman is a grand thing to see, for I'm told when Kitty Bawn was selling poteen below, the young men itself would never tire to be looking in her face.

MARTIN DOUL — *taking off his hat and feeling his head, speaking with hesitation.*— Did you think to look, Mary Doul, would there be a whiteness the like of that coming upon me?

MARY DOUL — *with extreme contempt.* — On you, God help you! . . . In a short while you'll have a head on you as bald as an old turnip you'd see rolling round in the muck. You need never talk again of your fine looks, Martin Doul, for the day of that talk's gone for ever.

MARTIN DOUL. That's a hard word to

be saying, for I was thinking if I'd a bit of comfort, the like of yourself, it's not far off we'd be from the good days went before, and that'd be a wonder surely. But I'll never rest easy, thinking you're a gray, beautiful woman, and myself a pitiful show.

MARY DOUL. I can't help your looks, Martin Doul. It wasn't myself made you with your rat's eyes, and your big ears, and your griseldy chin.

MARTIN DOUL — *rubs his chin ruefully, then beams with delight.*— There's one thing you've forgot, if you're a cute thinking woman itself.

MARY DOUL. Your slouching feet, is it? Or your hooky neck, or your two knees is black with knocking one on the other?

MARTIN DOUL — *with delighted scorn.* — There's talking for a cute woman. There's talking, surely!

MARY DOUL — *puzzled at joy of his voice.*— If you'd anything but lies to say you'd be talking to yourself.

MARTIN DOUL — *bursting with excitement.*— I've this to say, Mary Doul. I'll be letting my beard grow in a short while, a beautiful, long, white, silken, streamy beard, you wouldn't see the like of in the eastern world.. . . . Ah, a white beard's a grand thing on an old man, a grand thing for making the quality stop and be stretching out their hands with good silver or gold, and a beard's a thing you'll never have, so you may be holding your tongue.

MARY DOUL — *laughing cheerfully.*— Well, we're a great pair, surely, and it's great times we'll have yet, maybe, and great talking before we die.

MARTIN DOUL. Great times from this day, with the help of the Almighty God, for a priest itself would believe the lies of an old man would have a fine white beard growing on his chin.

MARY DOUL. There's the sound of one of them twittering yellow birds do be coming in the spring-time from beyond the sea, and there'll be a fine warmth now in the sun, and a sweetness in the air, the way it'll be a grand thing to be sitting here quiet and easy smelling the things growing up, and budding from the earth.

MARTIN DOUL. I'm smelling the furze a while back sprouting on the hill, and if you'd hold your tongue you'd hear the lambs of Grianan, though it's near drowned their crying is with the full river making noises in the glen.

MARY DOUL — *listens.* — The lambs is bleating, surely, and there's cocks and laying hens making a fine stir a mile off on the face of the hill. (*She starts.*)

MARTIN DOUL. What's that is sounding in the west?

[*A faint sound of a bell is heard.*

MARY DOUL. It's not the churches, for the wind's blowing from the sea.

MARTIN DOUL — *with dismay.* — It's the old Saint, I'm thinking, ringing his bell.

MARY DOUL. The Lord protect us from the saints of God! (*They listen.*) He's coming this road, surely.

MARTIN DOUL — *tentatively.* — Will we be running off, Mary Doul?

MARY DOUL. What place would we run?

MARTIN DOUL. There's the little path going up through the sloughs. . . . If we reached the bank above, where the elders do be growing, no person would see a sight of us, if it was a hundred yeomen were passing itself; but I'm afeard after the time we were with our sight we'll not find our way to it at all.

MARY DOUL — *standing up.*— You'd find the way, surely. You're a grand man the world knows at finding your way winter or summer, if there was deep snow in it itself, or thick grass and leaves, maybe, growing from the earth.

MARTIN DOUL — *taking her hand.*— Come a bit this way; it's here it begins. (*They grope about gap.*) There's a tree pulled into the gap, or a strange thing happened, since I was passing it before.

MARY DOUL. Would we have a right to be crawling in below under the sticks?

MARTIN DOUL. It's hard set I am to know what would be right. And isn't it a poor thing to be blind when you can't run off itself, and you fearing to see?

MARY DOUL — *nearly in tears.*— It's a poor thing, God help us, and what good'll our gray hairs be itself, if we have our sight, the way we'll see them falling each day, and turning dirty in the rain?

[*The bell sounds nearby.*

MARTIN DOUL — *in despair.*— He's coming now, and we won't get off from him at all.

MARY DOUL. Could we hide in the bit

of a briar is growing at the west butt of the church?

MARTIN DOUL. We'll try that, surely. (*He listens a moment.*) Let you make haste; I hear them trampling in the wood.

[*They grope over to church.*

MARY DOUL. It's the words of the young girls making a great stir in the trees. (*They find the bush.*) Here's the briar on my left, Martin; I'll go in first, I'm the big one, and I'm easy to see.

MARTIN DOUL — *turning his head anxiously.*— It's easy heard you are; and will you be holding your tongue?

MARY DOUL — *partly behind bush.*— Come in now beside of me. (*They kneel down, still clearly visible.*) Do you think they can see us now, Martin Doul?

MARTIN DOUL. I'm thinking they can't, but I'm hard set to know; for the lot of them young girls, the devil save them, have sharp, terrible eyes, would pick out a poor man, I'm thinking, and he lying below hid in his grave.

MARY DOUL. Let you not be whispering sin, Martin Doul, or maybe it's the finger of God they'd see pointing to ourselves.

MARTIN DOUL. It's yourself is speaking madness, Mary Doul; haven't you heard the Saint say it's the wicked do be blind?

MARY DOUL. If it is you'd have a right to speak a big, terrible word would make the water not cure us at all.

MARTIN DOUL. What way would I find a big, terrible word, and I shook with the fear; and if I did itself, who'd know rightly if it's good words or bad would save us this day from himself?

MARY DOUL. They're coming. I hear their feet on the stones.

[*The Saint comes in on right, with Timmy and Molly Byrne in holiday clothes, the others as before.*

TIMMY. I've heard tell Martin Doul and Mary Doul were seen this day about on the road, holy father, and we were thinking you'd have pity on them and cure them again.

SAINT. I would, maybe, but where are they at all? I have little time left when I have the two of you wed in the church.

MAT SIMON — *at their seat.*— There are the rushes they do have lying round on the stones. It's not far off they'll be, surely.

MOLLY BYRNE — *pointing with astonishment.*— Look beyond, Timmy.

[*They all look over and see Martin Doul.*

TIMMY. Well, Martin's a lazy fellow to be lying in there at the height of the day. (*He goes over shouting*) Let you get up out of that. You were near losing a great chance by your sleepiness this day, Martin Doul. . . . The two of them's in it, God help us all!

MARTIN DOUL — *scrambling up with Mary Doul.* — What is it you want, Timmy, that you can't leave us in peace?

TIMMY. The Saint's come to marry the two of us, and I'm after speaking a word for yourselves, the way he'll be curing you now; for if you're a foolish man itself, I do be pitying you, for I've a kind heart, when I think of you sitting dark again, and you after seeing a while and working for your bread.

[*Martin Doul takes Mary Doul's hand and tries to grope his way off right; he has lost his hat, and they are both covered with dust and grass seeds.*

PEOPLE. You're going wrong. It's this way, Martin Doul.

[*They push him over in front of the Saint, near centre. Martin Doul and Mary Doul stand with piteous hang-dog dejection.*

SAINT. Let you not be afeard, for there's great pity with the Lord.

MARTIN DOUL. We aren't afeard, holy father.

SAINT. It's many a time those that are cured with the well of the four beauties of God lose their sight when a time is gone, but those I cure a second time go on seeing till the hour of death. (*He takes the cover from his can.*) I've a few drops only left of the water, but, with the help of God, it'll be enough for the two of you, and let you kneel down now upon the road.

[*Martin Doul wheels round with Mary Doul and tries to get away.*

SAINT. You can kneel down here, I'm saying, we'll not trouble this time going to the church.

TIMMY — *turning Martin Doul round, angrily.*— Are you going mad in your head, Martin Doul? It's here you're to kneel. Did you not hear his reverence, and he speaking to you now?

SAINT. Kneel down, I'm saying, the ground's dry at your feet.

MARTIN DOUL — *with distress.*— Let you go on your own way, holy father. We're not calling you at all.

SAINT. I'm not saying a word of penance, or fasting itself, for I'm thinking the Lord has brought you great teaching in the blindness of your eyes; so you've no call now to be fearing me, but let you kneel down till I give you your sight.

MARTIN DOUL — *more troubled.*— We're not asking our sight, holy father, and let you walk on your own way, and be fasting, or praying, or doing anything that you will, but leave us here in our peace, at the crossing of the roads, for it's best we are this way, and we're not asking to see.

SAINT — *to the People.*— Is his mind gone that he's no wish to be cured this day, or to be living or working, or looking on the wonders of the world.

MARTIN DOUL. It's wonders enough I seen in a short space for the life of one man only.

SAINT — *severely.*— I never heard tell of any person wouldn't have great joy to be looking on the earth, and the image of the Lord thrown upon men.

MARTIN DOUL — *raising his voice.*— Them is great sights, holy father. . . . What was it I seen when I first opened my eyes but your own bleeding feet, and they cut with the stones? That was a great sight, maybe, of the image of God. . . . And what was it I seen my last day but the villainy of hell looking out from the eyes of the girl you're coming to marry — the Lord forgive you — with Timmy the smith. That was a great sight, maybe. And wasn't it great sights I seen on the roads when the north winds would be driving, and the skies would be harsh, till you'd see the horses and the asses, and the dogs itself, maybe, with their heads hanging, and they closing their eyes ——

SAINT. And did you never hear tell of the summer, and the fine spring, and the places where the holy men of Ireland have built up churches to the Lord? No man isn't a madman, I'm thinking, would be talking the like of that, and wishing to be closed up and seeing no sight of the grand glittering seas, and the furze that is opening above, and will soon have the hills shining as if it was fine creels of gold they were, rising to the sky.

MARTIN DOUL. Is it talking now you are of Knock and Ballavore? Ah, it's ourselves had finer sights than the like of them, I'm telling you, when we were sitting a while back hearing the birds and bees humming in every weed of the ditch, or when we'd be smelling the sweet, beautiful smell does be rising in the warm nights, when you do hear the swift flying things racing in the air, till we'd be looking up in our own minds into a grand sky, and seeing lakes, and big rivers, and fine hills for taking the plough.

SAINT — *to People.*— There's little use talking with the like of him.

MOLLY BYRNE. It's lazy he is, holy father, and not wanting to work; for a while before you had him cured he was always talking, and wishing, and longing for his sight.

MARTIN DOUL — *turning on her.*— I was longing, surely, for sight; but I seen my fill in a short while with the look of my wife, and the look of yourself, Molly Byrne, when you'd the queer wicked grin in your eyes you do have the time you're making game with a man.

MOLLY BYRNE. Let you not mind him, holy father; for it's bad things he was saying to me a while back — bad things for a married man, your reverence — and you'd do right surely to leave him in darkness, if it's that is best fitting the villainy of his heart.

TIMMY — *to Saint.*— Would you cure Mary Doul, your reverence, who is a quiet poor woman, never did hurt to any, or said a hard word, saving only when she'd be vexed with himself, or with young girls would be making game of her below.

SAINT — *to Mary Doul.*— If you have any sense, Mary, kneel down at my feet, and I'll bring the sight again into your eyes.

MARTIN DOUL — *more defiantly.*— You will not, holy father. Would you have her looking on me, and saying hard words to me, till the hour of death?

SAINT — *severely.*— If she's wanting her sight I wouldn't have the like of you stop her at all. (*To Mary Doul.*) Kneel down, I'm saying.

MARY DOUL — *doubtfully.*— Let us be as we are, holy father, and then we'll be known again in a short while as the people is happy and blind, and be having an easy time, with no trouble to live, and we getting halfpence on the road.

MOLLY BYRNE. Let you not be a raving fool, Mary Doul. Kneel down now, and let him give you your sight, and himself can be sitting here if he likes it best, and taking halfpence on the road.

TIMMY. That's the truth, Mary; and if it's choosing a wilful blindness you are, I'm thinking there isn't anyone in this place will ever be giving you a hand's turn or a hap'orth of meal, or be doing the little things you need to keep you at all living in the world.

MAT SIMON. If you had your sight, Mary, you could be walking up for him and down with him, and be stitching his clothes, and keeping a watch on him day and night the way no other woman would come near him at all.

MARY DOUL — *half persuaded.*— That's the truth, maybe ——

SAINT. Kneel down now, I'm saying, for it's in haste I am to be going on with the marriage and be walking my own way before the fall of night.

THE PEOPLE. Kneel down, Mary! Kneel down when you're bid by the Saint!

MARY DOUL — *looking uneasily towards Martin Doul.*— Maybe it's right they are, and I will if you wish it, holy father.

[*She kneels down. The Saint takes off his hat and gives it to some one near him. All the men take off their hats. He goes forward a step to take Martin Doul's hand away from Mary Doul.*

SAINT — *to Martin Doul.*— Go aside now; we're not wanting you here.

MARTIN DOUL — *pushes him away roughly, and stands with his left hand on Mary Doul's shoulder.*— Keep off yourself, holy father, and let you not be taking my rest from me in the darkness of my wife. . . . What call has the like of you to be coming between married people — that you're not understanding at all — and be making a great mess with the holy water you have, and the length of your prayers? Go on now, I'm saying, and leave us here on the road.

SAINT. If it was a seeing man I heard talking to me the like of that I'd put a black curse on him would weigh down his soul till it'd be falling to hell; but you're a poor blind sinner, God forgive you, and I don't mind you at all. (*He raises his can.*) Go aside now till I give the blessing to your wife, and if you won't go with your own will, there are those standing by will make you, surely.

MARTIN DOUL — *pulling Mary Doul.*— Come along now, and don't mind him at all.

SAINT — *imperiously, to the People.*— Let you take that man and drive him down upon the road.

[*Some men seize Martin Doul.*

MARTIN DOUL — *struggling and shouting.*— Make them leave me go, holy father!

Make them leave me go, I'm saying, and you may cure her this day, or do anything that you will.

SAINT — *to People.*— Let him be. . . . . Let him be if his sense is come to him at all.

MARTIN DOUL — *shakes himself loose, feels for Mary Doul, sinking his voice to a plausible whine.*— You may cure herself, surely, holy father; I wouldn't stop you at all — and it's great joy she'll have looking on your face — but let you cure myself along with her, the way I'll see when it's lies she's telling, and be looking out day and night upon the holy men of God.

[*He kneels down a little before Mary Doul.*

SAINT — *speaking half to the People.*— Men who are dark a long while and thinking over queer thoughts in their heads, aren't the like of simple men, who do be working every day, and praying, and living like ourselves; so if he has found a right mind at the last minute itself, I'll cure him, if the Lord will, and not be thinking of the hard, foolish words he's after saying this day to us all.

MARTIN DOUL — *listening eagerly.*— I'm waiting now, holy father.

SAINT — *with can in his hand, close to*

Martin Doul.— With the power of the water from the grave of the four beauties of God, with the power of this water, I'm saying, that I put upon your eyes ——

[*He raises can.*

MARTIN DOUL — *with a sudden movement strikes the can from the Saint's hand and sends it rocketing across stage. He stands up; People murmur loudly.*— If I'm a poor dark sinner I've sharp ears, God help me, and it's well I heard the little splash of the water you had there in the can. Go on now, holy father, for if you're a fine Saint itself, it's more sense is in a blind man, and more power maybe than you're thinking at all. Let you walk on now with your worn feet, and your welted knees, and your fasting, holy ways have left you with a big head on you and a thin pitiful arm. (*The Saint looks at him for a moment severely, then turns away and picks up his can. He pulls Mary Doul up.*) For if it's a right some of you have to be working and sweating the like of Timmy the smith, and a right some of you have to be fasting and praying and talking holy talk the like of yourself, I'm thinking it's a good right ourselves have to be sitting blind, hearing a soft wind turning round the little leaves of the spring and feeling the sun, and we not tormenting our souls with the sight of the gray days, and the holy men, and the dirty feet is trampling the world.

[*He gropes towards his stone with Mary Doul.*

MAT SIMON. It'd be an unlucky fearful thing, I'm thinking, to have the like of that man living near us at all in the townland of Grianan. Wouldn't he bring down a curse upon us, holy father, from the heavens of God?

SAINT — *tying his girdle.*— God has great mercy, but great wrath for them that sin.

THE PEOPLE. Go on now, Martin Doul. Go on from this place. Let you not be bringing great storms or droughts on us maybe from the power of the Lord.

[*Some of them throw things at him.*

MARTIN DOUL — *turning round defiantly and picking up a stone.*— Keep off now, the yelping lot of you, or it's more than one maybe will get a bloody head on him with the pitch of my stone. Keep off now, and let you not be afeard; for we're going on the two of us to the towns of the south, where the people will have kind voices maybe, and we won't know their bad looks or their villainy at all. (*He takes Mary Doul's hand again.*) Come along now and we'll be walking to the south, for we've seen too much of everyone in this place, and it's small joy we'd have living near them, or hearing the lies they do be telling from the gray of dawn till the night.

MARY DOUL — *despondingly.*— That's the truth, surely; and we'd have a right to be gone, if it's a long way itself, as I've heard them say, where you do have to be walking with a slough of wet on the one side and a slough of wet on the other, and you going a stony path with a north wind blowing behind. [*They go out.*

TIMMY. There's a power of deep rivers with floods in them where you do have to be lepping the stones and you going to the south, so I'm thinking the two of them will be drowned together in a short while, surely.

SAINT. They have chosen their lot, and the Lord have mercy on their souls. (*He rings his bell.*) And let the two of you come up now into the church, Molly Byrne and Timmy the smith, till I make your marriage and put my blessing on you all.

He turns to the church; procession forms, and the curtain comes down, as they go slowly into the church.

APPENDIX

THE WELL OF THE SAINTS was first produced in the Abbey Theatre in February, 1905, by the Irish National Theatre Society, under the direction of W. G. Fay, and with the following cast.

Martin Doul	W. G. FAY
Mary Doul	EMMA VERNON
Timmy	GEORGE ROBERTS
Molly Byrne	SARA ALLGOOD
Bride	MAIRE NIC SHIUBHLAIGH
Mat Simon	P. MAC SHIUBHLAIGH
The Saint	F. J. FAY

OTHER GIRLS AND MEN

THE ANDOVER PRESS
U. S. A.